PRAISE FOR
CHRISTOPHER HINZ

BINARY STORM

'This is a fast-paced future thriller that delivers on the promise of its high-concept premise.'
The B&N Sci-Fi & Fantasy Blog

"You'll want to hang in there for the entirety of the ride."
Strange Alliances

LIEGE KILLER

"It's a genuine page-turner, beautifully written and exciting from start to finish... Hinz presents this material with the assurance of classic sf and the vividness of the new masters... Don't miss it."
Locus

"Liege-Killer moves along at a brisk clip, providing one action-filled scene after another. Hinz writes with skill and verve. His world is logical and alive, and he peoples it with credible and compelling characters."
San Francisco Chronicle

ANGRY ROBOT
An imprint of Watkins Media Ltd

Unit 11, Shepperton House
89 Shepperton Road
London N1 3DF
UK

angryrobotbooks.com
twitter.com/angryrobotbooks
Mind blowing chess

An Angry Robot paperback original, 2019

Cover by Francesca Corsini
Set in Adobe Garamond

ISBN 978 0 85766 834 9
Ebook ISBN 978 0 85766 835 6

Printed and bound in the United Kingdom by TJ International.

9 8 7 6 5 4 3 2 1

CHRISTOPHER HINZ

DUCHAMP

♟ VERSUS ♚

EINSTEIN

ETAN ILFELD

ANGRY
ROBOT

DUCHAMP

28 July 1887
Duchamp born in Blainville-
Crevon, France

1912
Duchamp paints Nude
Descending a Staircase No. 2

1913
Armory Show (Art Show in
NYC)
First exhibition of modern art
in America

1917
Duchamp Submits Urinal to
an exhibition (Fountain)

1918
Duchamp arrives in Buenos
Aires, Argentina, and stays for
nine months

1927
Duchamp marries Lydie
Sarazin-Lavassor; however,
they divorce six months later

1932
Duchamp publishes a chess
book, Opposition and Sister
Squares are Reconciled

1954
Duchamp marries Alexina
"Teeny" Sattler

1955
Duchamp becomes a US
Citizen

2 October 1968
Duchamp dies in Neuilly-sur-
Seine, France

WORLD EVENTS

28 June 1914
Archduke Karl Ludwig
of Austria is assasinated
28 July 1914
World War I begins
15 August 1914
Panama Canal complete

11 Nov 1918
World War I ends
1 Sep 1939
World War II begins
16 July 1945
First Atomic Bomb test
(aka Trinity)
2 Sep 1945
World War II ends

EINSTEIN

14 March 1879
Einstein born in Ulm,
Germany

1896
Einstein renounces German
citizenship to avoid military
service and is stateless

1901
Einstein acquires Swiss
citizenship

1902
Joins the Swiss Patent office

1903
Marries Mileva Maric

1905
Publishes three seminal
papers: Theory of Special
Relativity; Photoelectric
effect, Brownian Motion

1911
Becomes an Austrian citizen
(which gradually changes
into German citizenship as
Austria joins Germany in the
following decades)

1919
Einstein divorces Mileva
Maric

1919
Einstein marries his cousin
Elsa Lowenthal

1921
Wins Nobel Prize in Physics

1933
Renounces German
citizenship and flees Germany

1936
Wife Elsa dies

1939
Einstein sends letter to
President Roosevelt about the
potential of atomic weapons

1940
Becomes an American citizen

19 April 1955
Einstein dies in Plainsboro,
New Jersey, USA

MANHATTAN, 1917

The newborn baby girl was more luminous and colorful than an Edison street lamp, more mysterious than the fragility of a winter's dawn. It materialized in front of Marcel Duchamp as he stood atop the Washington Square Arch, assuming form at the moment a swirling gust forced him to lean against the parapet for stability. The infant's multi-hued glow was reminiscent of a fiery sunrise – scarlets, magentas and raging ambers – with the illumination somehow emanating from deep within its tiny naked body.

Marcel's senses were momentarily numbed. The combination of icy January winds and surreal apparition floating in space just beyond the retaining wall stopped him from calling out in surprise to his fellow conspirators.

The hardened ground lay a good seventy-five feet beneath their perch atop the arch. In a rush of instinctive concern for the infant's safety, Marcel overcame his hesitation and reached out to grab it.

The infant disappeared – his hands encircled emptiness. He whirled in surprise to the conspirator nearest him along the parapet.

"Did you see that?"

"I see all, and thus am consumed by all misery," proclaimed drunken Gertrude Drick, spokeswoman for tonight's revolutionary act, as unyielding as a statue amid the fierce winds. A budding poet and self-proclaimed woman of anguish, Gertrude once distributed cards imprinted with the word *Woe* just so she could brag to friends and strangers that *Woe is me*.

Marcel, Gertrude and the other four conspirators had been up here for nearly an hour, insulating themselves against the cold of these wee morning hours with sandwiches and wine, and convivial appreciation for how much less illuminated the world would be without red Chinese lanterns, which they'd hung from the parapets to symbolize joy and good fortune.

"It's time," painter John Sloan announced. He waved to elicit the attention of the dozens of admirers gathered in the shadowy park at the foot of Fifth Avenue below, then signaled Gertrude with a nod. She positioned herself along the arch facing the gathering and slit the envelope. With a flourish, she withdrew the decree and commenced reading, her booming voice cleaving through the darkness like the foghorn of an East River freighter.

As Gertrude began the proclamation with a string of officious *whereases*, Marcel couldn't stop thinking about the glowing infant. Strange dream-like incidents had periodically touched him throughout his twenty-nine years. Yet until this moment, he'd never experienced what clearly must have been a mirage.

Was he drunk? Or during the beverage's fermentation, could some chemical have been unwittingly introduced that caused hallucinations? Nothing in the demeanor of the others indicated they were affected, although with Gertrude normally operating from a state of phantasmagoric zeal, evidence might be scant.

Marcel's attention returned to the "woman of woe" as she reached the heart of the matter, her vocal instrument rising to blustery heights as she announced that henceforth, Greenwich Village would be a free and independent republic.

Basking in the cheers of the crowd, the others fired cap pistols and released balloons to celebrate the liberation, and quaffed from pale bottles of purplish wine to give equal praise to libation. Marcel joined the merriment but halfheartedly, unable to remove his gaze from the spot where the infant had appeared and just as quickly dematerialized. Had what he'd witnessed been symbolic? A construct of his subconscious mind, an outpouring in the manner that Sigmund Freud had become famous for postulating?

"The time has come for our retreat," Gertrude proclaimed, lifting the trap door and leading them down the spiral staircase. "These heights will soon attract the repressive forces of the social order."

Marcel was glad to leave. The noises of freedom, particularly at such a late hour, likely would alert the police and result in prison. Hangovers would be more challenging to endure should they awaken to daylight in some dank Manhattan jail.

The movement provided an added bonus, relieving him, at least temporarily, of further thoughts of the infant. He followed the others through the access door at the base through which they had made their clandestine entrance. Admirers from the crowd surrounded them, generous with praise their slurred speech and swaying indicative of the frightfully drunk. Gertrude, John and the others, still consumed by radical fervor, took advantage of the alcohol-fueled admiration by plunging into rapid-fire conversation. Marcel's command of the American idiom remained imperfect in the two years since he'd come here from France, but he understood enough to grasp the main thread: Bohemian tirades against bourgeois sensibilities.

Declining an invitation to join the others at a nearby Irish tavern that never closed except on Christmas Eve and March 18, the day after the Feast of Saint Patrick,

Marcel bade them goodnight and began the long walk home. Escape failed to dispel his ongoing thoughts of the infant and what it might mean…

* * * * *

The following series of letters by Marcel Duchamp, translated from the artist's native French, were discovered hidden in the compartment of an early twentieth century desk in AD 2061. The desk was found within the sealed basement of a former New York City skyscraper, the site covered in five meters of atomic slag from the Manhattan Detonations. Noted World War III apocalyptic historian Trinita Rodriguez, the granddaughter of a woman born in Socorro, New Mexico, within minutes of the world's first atomic detonation – and a mere forty miles from ground zero – made the discovery. The original letters are on display at the W.M.D. wing of the Global Apocalypse Museum, Americana Colony, Luna.

Paris,
1st of August, 1914

Walter Arensberg
33 West 67th Street
New York City, NY, USA

My dear Walter,
Thank you for your recent letter and for the wonderful news and wishes. The

atmosphere in Paris is as silly as ever. Since the Archduke's assassination, the French leaders are amplifying the public's sense of panic, nationalism and xenophobia.

Political affairs aside, I must share with you the odd event that unfolded this week, which you might find amusing.

Despite a jubilant bash on Monday evening in celebration of my 27th birthday, I found it difficult to fall asleep that night. During the morning hours I was in a strange state, upon which I tried to ascertain if I was still dreaming or awake.

I keep an upside-down bicycle wheel mounted on a wooden stool at my studio and I gave the wheel a persuasive spin. As I waited for it to slowly grind to a halt, I noticed that it was maintaining its speed and momentum. At that moment my suspicions leaned toward the notion that I must be caught up in a dream.

I was determined to exert some sort of control over this apparent dream state. At first I jumped as high as I could, desiring to remain afloat, but disappointingly found that my body dropped back down to the floor as regularly as an apple would fall from a tree. Next, I walked over to the kitchen table, which still had yesterday's newspaper.

"Panama Canal Soon To Be Completed."

I shook the newspaper vigorously and discovered to my surprise that most of the letters of the headline became jumbled and rearranged into nonsensical gibberish. However, each time there would appear at least one legible word, including "sewer," "network" and several others that I cannot now recall. After a few more shuffles of the newspaper, I tired of this association game. For reasons that now elude me, I walked to my desk and wrote down a question addressed to what I assume was my subconscious:

"In a world that seems on the verge of great turmoil, what do I fear the most?"

I picked up the note, folded it in two and entered the bathroom. I dropped the note into the toilet bowl and yanked the chain to flush. After a few moments of swirling liquid, the paper disappeared into the subterranean depths, and at that moment I felt incredibly silly, as if my subconscious could be located in such a watery realm. But just as I was about to turn away, the note reappeared, gently bobbing on the surface of the freshly filled bowl. I retrieved the note and unfolded the paper, and was surprised to see that the drenching had caused the ink to spell out a new message:

"The masses, incest, the toxic smell of oil paint, determinism."

The retort, more than a bit cryptic, challenged my sensibilities. Still operating under the assumption that I was in a dream state, I jotted down a second query on another piece of paper:

"Who or what am I? What do I desire?"

I folded the note and flushed it, and was not terribly surprised to see it reappear. Fishing it from the toilet, I read it aloud.

"The energy of the night, imaginary stimuli, the chance to express myself, pleasure that can only be derived from bodily orifices."

Caught up in the throes of what was happening to me, I eagerly scrawled a third and final note. This time, I asked my subconscious, or whatever mystifying force was responding to my queries, something more specific:

"Should I travel to the Americas?"

In light of the unsettled events in Europe, and of a growing popularity of my work there, the question seemed appropriate.

The reply, by the same means already described, soon appeared.

"Go to New York City."

Before I could even consider further questions, my alarm clock began to ring. I found myself waking up in bed in a feverish sweat from what surely must have been a dream. Yet I had doubts about that. Was it instead an altered reality, a godlike transcendence? Does such a question even have an answer?

Most sincerely, and with regards to your dearest Louise,

Marcel Duchamp
23 St Hippolyte
Paris, France

MANHATTAN, 1917

Marcel's home was a modest bachelor's pad on 67th Street, on the west side of Central Park. To reach it from the Washington Square Arch, a three-and-a-half- mile walk up Fifth Avenue and Broadway was required. He certainly wasn't going to pay the exorbitant fare for one of those gasoline-powered taxis, whose drivers charged up to fifty cents a mile. Besides, he didn't mind long strolls through this easily navigable city at night. And a body in motion helped combat the cold.

He tightened the collar of his overcoat against the wind and pushed forward against a smattering of white flurries. The pavements were largely deserted, the cobblestone streets silent. Near 42nd Street, he saw and heard the quivering grunts and backfires of a milk truck that likely was causing its driver to curse all things mechanical and long for the serenity of horse-drawn vehicles. Despite the distraction, his thoughts kept circling back to the mysterious infant.

"How do you maintain your balance?"

The woman's voice surprised him. It seemed to ooze from a narrow alley, with a rectangular opening just high enough for someone of Marcel's stature to stand upright in. The shadowy alley was pinched between the grandiose staircases of two imposing brownstone residences.

He paused in his trek, unsure whether the words were directed at him. Perhaps the woman was speaking to a companion in the depths of the alley's impenetrable gloom, with reverberation producing an echo onto the street.

Hearing nothing further, Marcel continued on. But after only a few steps, the woman spoke again.

"Is it your custom to ignore an invitation to converse?"

His interest piqued, Marcel moved to the edge of the staircases flanking the alley. Possibilities flittered through his mind. The voice's owner could be a prostitute who had not yet earned her nightly keep and sought a final customer. Or perhaps she was a lady of higher social calling who, nonetheless, had drunk wine or liquor to the point of reduced inhibitions. A more ominous possibility was that the voice belonged to a siren in thrall to ruffians seeking to draw the unwary into the alley for robbery, or worse.

11

The nearest street lamp lacked enough illumination to penetrate the alley's mouth. Even standing this close, Marcel could make out nothing but a nest of shadows.

"Who are you?" he challenged. "What do you want?"

There was no response. Marcel decided the prudent choice was to ignore the disembodied voice. Once again, he turned away to continue his northward trek. Once again, her words brought him to a halt.

"You may call me… Stella. I witnessed your artistry at the Armory Show. Four years ago, was it not?"

He froze. Indeed, the first American appearance of his work had been at the 1913 International Exhibition of Modern Art, held in New York's 69th Regiment Armory. At the time, Marcel had still been in France. He had not learned until weeks after the opening that his painting, *Nude Descending a Staircase, No. 2*, had caused a furor and rendered him an instant celebrity in the American art world.

He retraced his steps back to the alley, more curious than ever about the identity and motives of the mysterious Stella. It was likely she wasn't a harlot, drunken socialite or the façade for some lowlife criminal enterprise.

But the strangeness of the encounter justified caution. He inched past the twin staircases until he was two paces from the alley's entrance. It was then that he realized there was something strange about the alley itself. It didn't look like it belonged. The rectangular perimeter possessed an odd blurriness that contrasted with the clear geometrical lines that defined the flanking brownstones. Marcel had wandered along many of Manhattan's streets but had never encountered such a passageway between homes. He peered into the depths, straining to comprehend shape within the gloom.

"Did you attend the Armory show?" he called out.

"I bore witness to it."

If the voice was attempting to heighten Marcel's curiosity, its ploy was excellent.

"Have we met before?" He had the oddest feeling that indeed they had, although a place and time remained elusive.

"We are meeting now," she replied.

"Why don't you come out of there?"

"Why don't you come in?"

Marcel's confusion grew. He didn't know what to make of this verbal sparring and remained in the grip of uneasiness. He couldn't shake the feeling that Stella represented some form of profound danger.

"I'd prefer to stay out here where the lighting is better and more conducive to friendly conversation."

"Light is not always what it seems."

He stepped closer, drawn by what seemed to be intelligence brimming beneath those words. He was now only a pace from the alley's mouth.

"Just one more step," she urged.

Marcel continued to hesitate, torn between fascination and apprehension.

"Fear does not become the man who, a few months hence, will purchase a porcelain urinal, inscribe it with a *nom de plume*, and deliver it anonymously to a Lexington Avenue hall with the hope of entering it – upside down – as a radical work of art in an exhibition."

Marcel was at a loss for words, a condition from which he seldom suffered, even when the conversation was in English and not his mother tongue. Was the woman some sort of gypsy soothsayer of the type he'd occasionally encountered in Paris? If so, her confident prediction of future events would be followed by a financial request. The solicitation might involve a sad tale of familial suffering, perhaps relatives detained on nearby Ellis Island who were in need of assistance to make the final leap into America's promise.

"I have no money," Marcel said. The statement was untrue. On this night he carried six bits, a combination of nickels and dimes. The coins were enshrouded in a handkerchief in his trouser pocket to stop them from rattling so as not to entice thieves.

"I do not seek money."

"Nevertheless, I feel more comfortable remaining out here." He paused, not wanting her to know he was afraid, and forced a smile. "But I have no problem continuing our verbal chess match."

There was a long pause on her part, as if she was giving special consideration to his remarks.

"Chess," she said finally, endowing the word with a strong emphasis. "The warlike confrontation inherent in the game would seem foreign to the creator of such artistic abstractions."

"To be human is to be confronted with dualities," he countered, aware that his response also served as an appropriate answer to her initial question about how he maintained his balance.

There was another pause as she mulled over his answer.

"Do you play chess?" he asked.

"I do not. But I know that you are enticed by the game. Therefore, allow me to offer a trade. Enter my domain and I will arrange a chess match the likes of which you will never have experienced."

Given the circumstances, the proposal was strange if not outright ludicrous. Yet somehow, Marcel believed her. Intrigued to the point of overcoming trepidation, he stepped into the shadows and reached out his hand. His fingers brushed against something that inexplicably felt both solid and ethereal. At that instant, in his mind's eye, he again perceived the glowing infant.

"The baby is yours!" he uttered, astonished by the conclusion he had come to.

Marcel's world exploded.

A barrage of heat and light swept over him, hurling him backward amid a shock wave of tingling energy. For an instant, it felt as if every muscle in his body was connected to a powerful electric current.

The sensation vanished and he slammed hard onto his back out in the street.

Overcoming his shock, he righted himself and brushed splotches of dirt from his coat. Other than a few sore spots where the rippled cobblestones had bruised, he didn't seem injured.

What had happened? Had a bomb gone off? Had Stella been one of those mad assassins who blew themselves up in the name of some arcane political belief? Had she been attempting to entice him into the alley to carry out an assassination?

It seemed a reasonable scenario. Considering his minor flirtation with American fame, surely there would be more prominent newspaper coverage of the bombing. The killing of Marcel Duchamp would mean more than the mere self-annihilation of some unknown radical.

Those questions and more bubbled through his mind as he tried to make sense of it all. However, when he returned his attention to the alley, there were no traces of the explosion, neither shattered windows nor scattered debris. Far stranger, there was no evidence of the alley itself. A solid wall joined the brownstones. Stella, had she ever existed, was gone.

* * * * *

She was a creation apart. A non-participant occupying a realm beyond what organic lifestreams perceived as the knowable universe. Coursing through nonlinear dimensions while cradled in a perpetual observational context, she bore witness to the lifestreams' pasts and futures, observed their brief journeys from birth to cessation.

Only a few species of lifestreams ascended the three-rung evolutionary ladder to become Tripartites, progressing from pure physicality to emotional awareness to cerebral intelligence. Most of those who achieved the third rung of self-awareness developed coherent civilizations, but it was the exceptions that interested her – the Anomalous Tripartites, she called them – those species whose physical, emotional and intellectual components smoldered in perpetual conflict. Her own existence – predictable, secure, largely unaffected by spatiotemporal events – lacked contradictions, whereas Anomalous Tripartites possessed it in abundance. She perused this rarer subset with the scholarly dedication of the outsider, yet with a specific purpose in mind.

The latest expulsion was coming. An amalgamation was required.

Early in her research, she focused on a species of blue-skinned insectoids who fashioned subterranean chambers. Their world's surface had been rendered a radioactive wasteland by another Anomalous Tripartite species that had self- destructed eons earlier.

The insectoids scavenged technological junk from the departed civilization and refashioned it into nonfunctional sculptures, cramming the sculptures into their underground abodes. The highest social standing was given to individuals who acquired so much junk they no longer had living space. At that juncture, cheered on by family and friends, they abandoned their homes for ritualistic climbs to the surface, where they soon perished from radiation poisoning.

She next turned her attention to an equally strange species, oily amphibians fascinated with all things genealogical. The amphibians occupied a hot, seismically unstable planet that suffered perpetual quakes. They compensated for the instability by constructing floating swamp cities to buffer the turbulence. Each city was built near a volcanic vent that expelled magma-heated water into a bubbling thermal pool, and many amphibians claimed to see the faces of ancestors within these cauldrons, beckoning them to a better world. A popular social activity, as well as a voluntary form of population control, was diving into the pools to be scalded to death.

But of all the Anomalous Tripartites she studied, none seemed as steeped in the anomalous as a species of fleshy bipedals living aboveground on the land masses of a world three-quarters aquatic. Although the bipedals sometimes committed suicide, in general it was not a socially sanctioned activity as it was for the insectoids and the amphibians, where voluntary termination achieved high status.

The bipedals had developed their own unique means for assuring high casualty rates. By banding together in large groups, called "nations", and fighting brutal wars with others in the name of freedom, for the acquisition of resources or for the placation or worship of beloved deities, they existed in a state of near-constant strife. Their wars tended to enhance the power and wealth of the nations' ruling classes, a concept to which the majority of those directly impacted by the combat remained blissfully unenlightened.

Yet it was not their overall belligerence that intrigued her but the strident uniqueness possessed by a tiny percentage. These aberrations defied social conventions and served as counterweights to the warfare-encrusted majority.

A decision was reached. She would select the amalgamation from among the species known as "humans".

* * * * *

Marcel Duchamp
23 St. Hippolyte
Paris, France

9th of August, 1914

Walter Arensberg
33 West 67th Street
New York City, NY, USA

My dear Walter,

A strong urge prompted me to compose this follow-up letter to the one I sent you last week, which I hope you have received and digested by now. It concerns what occurred a few days after the events I previously described to you, namely, another journey into mysterious realms.

I had been staffing the reference desk at the Saint- Genevieve Library while reading Poincare's <u>Science and Hypothesis</u>, and in a moment of wandering attention from the text, I recalled having read somewhere that the physicist Albert Einstein read this very work a year before he published his special theory of relativity in 1905. Poincare, in less mathematical terms than Einstein, ingeniously asserts that there is no such thing as absolute time or, for that matter, absolute truth.

I then began to reminisce about the first time I had met Einstein, during my visit to Prague in 1912. It was during an afternoon at Bertha Fanta's literary salon that I encountered him, in conversation with a writer by the surname of Kafka. No ordinary chap himself, Kafka was vigorously debating with Einstein about whether the use of an omniscient narrator in literature implied the existence of a higher power.

The debate was in German, but I was fortunate enough to be in the company of a translator and so able to follow most of it. At several points, I desired to add my own thoughts to the debate, yet held back for fear of being seen as an interloper. But finally, with an invigoration of courage and the assistance of the translator, I jumped into the fray.

I suggested that there is no such thing as a definitive verdict - only a momentary point of view - and that even God must have his own army of bureaucrats.

Einstein and Kafka accepted my incursion with agreeable nods, then returned to their animated discussion.

And it was at that moment, my dearest Walter, that the world again went strange. Lo and behold, a waking dream - at least I think it was a dream - swept me away, and I found myself in a labyrinth of administrative officials, each hard at work at a typewriter. I attempted to ask several of them where the exit was from this perplexing maze within which they performed their duties, but they merely hushed me while averting their gazes. After several minutes of walking helplessly in circles, I decided to try something more extreme to get their attention.

I jumped onto one of the desks, kicked the typewriter to the floor and began to undress. The official utilizing the desk reacted to my display by standing up and walking swiftly in a direction I had not yet attempted in my efforts to escape. I hopped off the desk and followed him, but mysteriously soon found myself alone. I was in a large hallway flanked by windows interspersed with bizarre paintings, ranging from undecipherable montages of famed cultural icons to a gigantic portrait of a yellow frog in a tropical forest.

And then occurred the strangest part of this already strange experience. A woman appeared. She was stunning; tall, blonde and slim, and wearing a long dress that initially seemed to be made from some uncommon black material, perhaps some variant of silk. But as a shaft of morning light appeared through one of the windows, her dress brightened into a dazzling array of fierce colors, ever-changing blends of red, gold and violet. It was as if the dress was composed of the very heart of a great dawn.

She smiled at me from a few paces away, and spoke in a voice seemingly both lyrical and ordinary.

"You will consider a game of chess."

For a moment I did not know how to respond.

"I am not thinking of now," she clarified. "I am thinking of then."

"Then?" I asked.

"So be it," she said, in a tone that suggested the two of us had just settled something of great importance.

At that moment, for reasons unknown, my thoughts returned to the previous week's evening chess bout with Picabia, which as usual had featured a heated debate about the future of art, with Francis adamantly claiming that New York City was the place to be, that it was a metropolis with a younger and more subversive sensibility than other global communities. I was not so certain, and argued against it. In the end, we did agree on one thing. Many of Europe's young artists will be creatively and physically handicapped by military conscription, making the New World all the more enticing compared to the morbid dourness of Europe.

"A final question," the woman said. "Would you prefer to live underwater?"

It was precisely at that moment that I was awakened by church bells ringing from across the street. I was surprised to find that I had nodded off at the reference desk of the Saint-Genevieve

Library, with <u>Science and Hypothesis</u> plopped in my lap.

This event was the end, or nearly the end, of these several days of unusual experiences. One more odd thing happened however, about an hour after I had awakened. A customer approached me at the reference desk and asked if I had a book about tropical amphibians.

Clearly, life can be as strange as a dream. Clearly, everything can be a form of art.

Most sincerely, and with regards as always to your dearest Louise,

Marcel Duchamp
23 St Hippolyte
Paris, France

MANHATTAN, 1917

By the time Marcel arrived at his apartment he'd churned over the mysterious incident to the point of distraction, and upon entering, he tripped over one of his own works of arts and landed face down on the floor. The object that had snagged his ankle was, appropriately enough, named the *Trebuchet*, from the French verb meaning "to trip." In reality it was a wall-mountable coat rack – four metal brackets on a wooden support – that he'd never gotten around to hanging up.

After stumbling over the coat rack on several occasions, he'd decreed that it deserved Readymade status. Like his other Readymades, *Trebuchet* had been chosen on the basis of it being a mass-produced object severely lacking esthetic qualities. Representing neither good taste nor bad taste, it simply *was*. With that criterion in mind, he'd nailed it to the floor.

Righting himself from this latest fall – the second one in the past half hour – he entered the bathroom to wash up. The toilet beside the sink reminded him of Stella's prediction that he would buy a urinal and promote it as a legitimate art piece. In reality, he indeed had considered just such a purchase several weeks ago while walking past a Fifth Avenue iron works and seeing a Bedfordshire-model urinal on display. Such a piece would provoke strong reactions while representing the network of sewage systems that functioned as the bloodstream of civilization.

But what had really occurred back at the alley-that-wasn't-an-alley? Had any aspect of his bizarre encounter with the woman been real? And what about the glowing infant, who he remained certain was Stella's offspring? The two incidents must have a deeper connection than Marcel could fathom. Or had he simply been caught up in a lengthy hallucinatory state due to , overindulgence in revolutionary fervor or tiredness?

The latter interpretations held appeal. But as he splashed cold water on his face and scrubbed his hands with a coarse sliver of soap, a true explanation seemed as far beyond his grasp as the liquid swirling into the depths of the sink's drain.

* * * * *

Utilizing a chronobiological scan across 50,000 human years and a selection process infused with both rationality and randomness, she chose an individual for more intimate exploration. Examining the lifestream from birth to death, she narrowed her range of interest to a year that his species reckoned as AD 1917, in a nation called the United States of America, in a place called New York City.

The United States was at that time on the cusp of entering a conflagration that had enveloped many nations on another continent, a so-called Great War that would result in more than sixteen million dead. For bipedals, that represented an above-average casualty figure for a single conflict. Historically impressive as it was for them, however, the number would be greatly exceeded within most of their lifetimes by a second global war.

The individual she selected was a man who created art that confounded sensibilities, even the sensibilities of someone like herself, whose tastes were forged from the observation of millions of lifestreams over countless millennia.

She was struck by Nude Descending a Staircase, No. 2, *and the shattered composition sandwiched between pieces of glass referred to as* The Bride Stripped Bare By Her Bachelors, Even. *Those creations, among others, blended the sensible and the nonsensical in unexpected ways. They straddled a fence separating sanity from madness, somehow maintaining their balance in the face of relentless turbulence.*

She further narrowed her scan to a particular spatiotemporal locus early in that year of 1917, to a windswept Manhattan street on a cold January morning prior to sunrise. An incursion into a lifestream carried a degree of risk, not only for herself and the subject, but potentially for the lifestream's entire species. However, corporeal interaction seemed the only sensible way to proceed. And Henri-Robert-Marcel Duchamp seemed an excellent first target for the amalgamation.

BERN, 1905

Working as an examiner at the patent office in Bern, Switzerland, was less than challenging. Albert Einstein found much of the work mechanical and routine. The quality of submissions to his office varied greatly, and although many of them at least were straightforward, they too often were accompanied by engineering schematics and explanations woefully lacking in imagination.

Albert had finished his physics studies in 1901 but was unable to find an academic position. He was grateful to get paid work that at least utilized a modicum of intelligence. Here at the Bern Federal Office for Intellectual Property, his specialty was evaluating patents relating to the transmission of electrical signals and the synchronization of time.

The most boring submissions tended to be harebrained replications of devices already in existence. Many of those could be further classified into the subcategory of "inventions likely to prompt litigation by rightful patent owners". Still, on occasion, applications suggested at least an attempt to create something novel, such as the recent entry whereby a stationary bicycle was linked to a sewing machine, with the operator's steady rotation of the pedals actuating an electric generator that powered a rhythmically thrusting needle.

But the submissions he enjoyed most were those that audaciously sidestepped or challenged the social norms. Albert prided himself on maintaining an open and liberal attitude, something that could be said of the Swiss in general, at least when compared to those narrow minds increasingly common in his native Germany. The best of those submissions that evaded the status quo could also spark amusement, even occasional bouts of laughter. For reasons that Albert could not adequately explain, the analysis of such items often made the day seem to go faster. It was as if they caused time itself to flow at a different rate.

He had been asked to process one such elegant and amusing entry only yesterday, from the Zurich Electrical Supply Company. The firm's banana-shaped Premium Vibrator was ostensibly a device for general feminine relaxation and improved health. The applicant claimed, in a barrage of pseudoscientific language that artfully avoided the device's more titillating potential, that it was intended for face, scalp and body massage, and that regular use engendered remarkable curative properties. Not only would headaches and wrinkles be eliminated, but the vibrator also held out the promise of perpetual youth. And because it plugged into the common outlet – *just like your electric lamp*, the accompanying advertisement proclaimed – it was said to be quieter and free of the dense clouds of smoke that plagued steam-powered models.

Albert had become a permanent employee at the patent office two years ago. Although technically having to spend at least eight hours a day at his desk, he often was able to finish his allotment of tasks at a swifter pace than his coworkers. The remainder of the workday could then be applied to his true passion: dwelling on the mathematical laws of the universe and writing research papers in support of his calculations and conclusions.

He was engaged in just that activity on this warm afternoon in May 1905, shortly after a thunderstorm had soaked the area. He was alone, planted firmly on a shaded park bench near his office, a selection of local newsprint serving as a barrier between his posterior and the damp bench slats. He'd completed his duties for the day, including an hour squeezed in for his studies. Now, before heading home to wife Mileva and their year-old son Hans, he was taking a few moments to find a solution to a stubborn problem he'd been dwelling on for seven years.

How exactly did relative motion impact the phenomena of electromagnetism?

An answer at times seemed tantalizingly within reach. Yet whenever he completed the calculations, they produced mathematical dead-ends. Recently, he'd begun to experience a sense of despair that the problem could be solved.

As he was churning the idea and a corresponding stream of calculations around in his head, trying to approach a solution from yet another perspective, he reached for the cloth bag at his side. It contained his leftovers from lunch. A small loaf of bread and bottle of milk had already been consumed but a ripe golden apple remained. He'd intended to save it for tomorrow's lunch but reconsidered, believing that perhaps its jolt of sugar might pump new energy into his brain.

As his hand crept into the bag and grasped the apple, a woman sat down on the far side of the bench, just beyond his reaching arm. He was so startled by her abrupt appearance from nowhere that he wrenched his hand from the lunch bag. That caused the apple to roll off the bench and fall, with Newtonian certainty, onto a patch of moist grass at his feet.

Albert reached down to retrieve the fallen fruit. Not wishing to be impolite and eat in front of a stranger, he returned it to the bag.

"How do you maintain your balance?"

The woman spoke in Albert's native German. Something about her precise yet lyrical tone made him think that she might be a singer, or perhaps a visiting actress in the employ of one of those touring theater companies.

He could think of no appropriate response to the oddly phrased greeting. Yet it was more than just her words that rendered him silent. In the brief moment he had looked away from her to gather up the fallen fruit, her very appearance seemed to have changed.

At first glance, her dark hair and round face had brought to mind Mileva. But now she seemed to have transformed into a younger woman, no more than twenty years of age, with a slim attractive figure and flowing wheat-colored hair that reminded him of an autumnal field. Indeed, her new incarnation was possessed of such rare and dazzling beauty that the few remnants of calculations and probabilities having to do with relative motion and electromagnetism still churning through Albert's head were swept away.

He was well aware that such a startling metamorphosis could not have occurred.

A quick analysis of the situation produced the only rational answer. Beneath Albert's consciousness of the moment, he had been thinking about going home to his wife. Thus upon first laying eyes on the woman, his mind had played a trick. He had perceived the woman from a perspective at odds with reality.

Having recently come across several articles published by a fascinating Viennese doctor named Freud, such self-deceptions seemed well within the realm of the believable.

"Is it your custom to ignore an invitation to converse?" she asked in response to his silence.

"Of course not," he offered in an apologetic tone. "It's just that you surprised me."

She lifted her gaze to the canopy of a distant forest. "It is within my nature to have such tendencies."

Albert found her response infernally odd. He took closer notice of her attire, having initially gauged her long dress as sewn out of a silk-like material, dyed black. Yet as the late afternoon sun crept through the treetops and fell upon it, the fabric displayed an alternating range of hues depending on the angle the sunlight struck it. He glimpsed flashes of scarlet in the material, then a series of yellow-greens reminiscent of grasslands aflame, and finally a selection of mauves and violets. It appeared as if the dress bore the capability of streaming through the entire spectrum of visible light, with a preponderance of colors he associated with the breaking of dawn. But that should not be possible. No dressmaking material with which he was familiar could possibly offer such an extraordinary range of hues.

A suspicion formed that things were not as they seemed. Could he be so addled by her ethereal beauty that he was hallucinating? Or perhaps something more fundamental had occurred and he'd fallen asleep on the bench, and was now the throes of a dream.

"This is not a dream," she said, as if reading his thoughts.

"What proof is there of that?" he demanded, frustration slipping into his words. He couldn't fathom exactly what was going on and felt that he was suddenly in the midst of a situation that defied logic. Yet simultaneously he realized that his frustration had little to do with the mysterious woman. The vexation's true cause was his seven-year inability to solve the problem of relative motion's impact on electromagnetism.

"Who are you?" he asked, recapturing his poise.

"You may call me… Stella. What would you say to a game of chess?"

Surprised by the change of subject, Albert again found himself at a loss for words. He played the game rarely these days, and then only with Mileva. His wife's background in applied physics, geometry and mechanics made her an effective chess opponent.

"I have little time for such things," he finally responded. "And unless you're carrying one of those miniature chessboards in your purse, the question remains theoretical."

"I am not inviting you to play a game at this moment. I was thinking of another time. Another place. Another opponent."

He stared in fascination at the collar of her dress, which seemed to be transforming from a vibrant shade of amber to a pulsating crimson. She offered a fresh smile, so dazzling that it filled the air with crisscrossing shafts of white light of such intensity that Albert momentarily had to close his eyes. The illumination seemed to have physical form, as if composed of both waves and particles.

"You appear to emit your own light," he stated.

"Light is not always what it seems."

In any other setting, Albert would never be so rude as to put his hands on a woman without her consent. But the ethereal strangeness of what was happening demanded action. He was feeling increasingly unhinged, like a thunderbolt desperate to seek an electrical ground, to seek earth.

He reached out to touch her shoulder. His fingers made contact...

And the world exploded. A barrage of heat and light knocked him violently sideways off the bench. His backside touched down first, on a patch of wet grass. He struggled to his feet, relieved to be uninjured, with the possible exception of his pride.

The intense light had vanished and with it, the woman. There was no sign of her anywhere. The only other individuals present in the park were an elderly couple passing beneath an oak tree some twenty meters away. Albert smoothed his rumpled jacket and brushed leaves from the seat of his pants and dashed over to them.

"That woman who was with me," he asked breathlessly. "Did you happen to notice where she went?"

The couple's response only heightened the mystery. Both claimed to have seen Albert on the bench as they strolled past but no one else. They did admit that they thought it rather odd that he appeared to have been talking to himself.

Albert offered a mumbled "thank you" and returned to the bench. The bag with his apple was all that remained to mark the location of the strange incident.

What had happened? Why had the elderly couple noticed nothing out of the ordinary except for Albert vigorously conversing with an invisible presence? How could that be? How could one person perceive something happening in a certain space at a certain time, while other observers experienced an entirely different view relative to the same event?

Stunned by the impact of the encounter, by the woman's cryptic words and perplexing appearance and disappearance, Albert headed for home. Yet however irrational the incident had been, he was suddenly filled with great excitement, of the sort that accompanied fresh discovery. The seed of an idea had been planted. He could feel it tumbling about within the deepest recesses, on the tantalizing edge of consciousness.

Light is not always what it seems, Stella had said. The notion triggered a flow of equations in his head. He felt as if her presence was the harbinger of a theory that, with just a bit more mental effort, might well illuminate the darkness.

* * * * *

Marcel Duchamp
Nice, France

15th of March, 1928

Alfred Stieglitz
Room 303, Anderson Gallery
Park Avenue and 59th Street
New York, NY, USA

My dear Alfred,

Thank you for the wedding gift, and for your marvelous letter. I hope that O'Keeffe is recovering from her operation, and that your lovely wife's paintings remain lucrative.

You may be surprised to hear that I am now living in Nice as a bachelor and that my divorce from Lydie was finalized in January. She was more threatened by my chess pieces than by other women. Surely, one can love different things in equal measure without contradiction. Is that how you feel for both Georgia and Dorothy? Out of jealousy, Lydie glued my Staunton set to its board. I knew then that we could no longer be husband and wife.

The divorce has already done me good: I won an international chess tournament last month in Hyères. The game allows me to indulge in a purely mental state where I can think, strategize and create new sequences. Having known many artists and chess players, I have come to the conclusion that while all artists are not chess players, all chess players are artists.

When I win a beautiful game, I feel a sense of enlightenment that my art has never matched. I must continue seeking out stronger opponents to nourish my skills. The only thing that could stimulate my interest right now is a wonder drug that would make me play chess divinely. That would really excite me.

I have tried grinding chocolate with various pharmaceuticals and herbs, but have yet to discover any significant effects.

A disdain for chess is not a universal quality of the fair sex. Even the structure of chess is predisposed towards the dominating queen who hunts the vulnerable crusading king. This brings to mind the events of about ten years ago, shortly after that memorable night in Manhattan, when revolutionary fervor seemed to lead to extraordinary incidents.

I was living in Buenos Aires where I had a series of sensual chess encounters with an enigmatic woman who called herself Estrella. Buenos Aires is dull at night and there was little to do other than work on art or visit the local chess club. Estrella was enchanting, and made for a formidable opponent, as I had not yet mastered the royal game.

The first time we met, we played until the club closed in the early hours of the following morning. We played lightning chess with only a few minutes for each game, and had gone through at least half a dozen games, with me winning the most. The victories brought additional satisfaction as she had mentioned that she would only sleep with men who could beat her at chess.

Afterwards, we made our way to my apartment where we continued to play with the added consequence that the loser of each lightning game removed an article of clothing. An hour later, she was left wearing only a silky black chemise, while I had only removed my jacket and socks. The sight of her beauty served to diminish my concentration however, and thirty minutes later, I too was almost nude. Our mental foreplay soon led to a more physical exchange.

Estrella was an inspiration and shared with me her explorations of automatic writing, alchemical formulas and mesmerism. During our chess games she would often roll an eight-sided die to decide which pawn to move first. In some indeterminable way, her strange habits and interests served to remind me of the mysterious Stella

I'd encountered in Manhattan – or perhaps only encountered in dream and hallucination – a woman who seemed able to predict aspects of my future.

Predicting the future is difficult in chess and all but impossible in life, at least for those of us constrained by the dimensions of mortality. However, I will make a prophecy that I shall not paint again. But thank you for proposing another exhibition. I suggest that you pursue Picabia. He is not a fake like most others, and I will gladly make an introduction for you when I am in Paris next month.

Affectionately yours,
Marcel Duchamp
Grand Cafe de la Poste
Place Wilson et 25
Rue Hotel-des-Postes
Nice, France

* * * * *

Even for an outsider such as herself, the universe obeyed rules. From the randomly subatomic to the astronomically immense, order was maintained.

Until it wasn't.

43

She'd enticed Marcel Duchamp and Albert Einstein to venture close. Luring them had introduced a level of uncertainty into an inherently unstable situation. During her numerous previous incursions into AT civilizations she always tried limiting herself to dialogue – an intellectual exchange of ideas – since touching a lifestream carried the risk of being ensnared by it.

Of course her strategy of detachment perpetually failed. An amalgamation was a necessary predecessor to an expulsion and required a form of solidity that her isolated existence could not offer. She chose not to examine too closely the fact that she endlessly repeated the identical pattern of events and that the end result was always the same, being wrenched from her pure observational context.

No longer a mere observer of the knowable universe she was caught up in it, snared in a state of faux-physicality. She was trapped within Duchamp and Einstein's spheres of influence, trapped within a realm of finite yesterdays and tomorrows.

MANHATTAN, 1917

It was nearly noon when Marcel awoke. A good night's sleep hadn't alleviated his anxiety over the previous night's encounter with the mysterious woman who called herself Stella, as well as with the equally cryptic manifestation of the newborn infant atop the arch. And did that invitation to a future chess game possess some significance he couldn't decipher?

A fantastical idea occurred as he lay there in bed. His interest in the game of kings preceded both ethereal encounters, having grown up in a family that enjoyed playing chess. What if Stella somehow had been the one to inspire his early interest in the game?

Einstein was said to have shown that time was relativistic, and he sensed that in some fundamental way, Stella was not bound by the rules of the temporal. Could she have arranged to appear within the depths of his Normandy childhood, perhaps as a dream or hallucination, so far back that his thought processes were still too infantile to shape meaning? Had she inexorably enticed him toward a passion for guiding sixteen-piece armies on boards of sixty-four squares?

He shook his head in denial and hopped out of bed. Such ideas were madness.

Strolling through Central Park a short time later on his way to a rendezvous, he felt as if he'd recovered from the strange events. Still, in the back of his mind lurked a suspicion that the encounter with Stella had somehow detoured him into a fundamentally altered reality, onto a path distinct from where the rest of the world tread.

A portly man in a dark navy overcoat waved at Marcel from a park bench, thankfully distracting him from a further rehash. He was to provide the man's son with French lessons in exchange for a tidy sum of coins. It would be enough money so that if he ever again found himself confronted with the choice of walking Manhattan streets in the wee hours of the morning or hailing a taxi, he would have the economic wherewithal to elect the latter course.

* * * * *

Never had she found herself imprisoned within a pair of lifestreams simultaneously. She was intrigued by the possibilities her predicament afforded – unprecedented physical and emotional interaction with two members of an Anomalous Tripartite species. Yet she was concerned that she might never be able to return to her observational context.

Although trapped, she maintained a certain freedom of spatiotemporal movement. Her essence could navigate across the face of the planet, the same capability with which Duchamp and Einstein were endowed. In terms of human timekeeping, the artist's existence went from 1887 to 1968, and the scientist's from 1879 to 1955, which meant she could move freely across the breadth of those years. Any such leaps within that span would leave temporal wakes, possibly causing phantom traces of her thoughts and intentions to appear in the dreams and imaginations of sensitive humans.

Although she doubted that any human remained completely immune to the inherent warlike tendencies of their species, Duchamp and Einstein's interest in chess would seem to indicate that their physical and emotional selves, the sources of much of their propensity to warfare, had been subsumed beneath an intellectual stratum. They might engage in a rational form of combat via the game, thereby avoiding the havoc of the genuine article.

That led her to configure a plan. It was one that not only would fulfill her requirements in regard to the expulsion and enable her to escape the limitations of this locus, but also allow for a deeper exploration of physicality and emotionality.

LONG ISLAND, 1939

Albert's second season in Cutchogue, Long Island, should have been as enjoyable as his first. But recent events had accelerated the worrisome situation in Germany. That madman Hitler's lust to conquer and destroy seemed to possess no upper limit. Last November's anti-Jewish pogrom had been awful enough. This year, his renouncing of non-aggression pacts with Poland and Britain suggested worse.

It was a warm evening, this first Tuesday in August, although not unbearably so.

Albert had opened all the screened windows in the tidy cottage he rented on Old Cove Road, which was only a few hundred feet from Little Peconic Bay. Those waters constituted the most beautiful sailing ground he'd ever experienced.

Wednesday's forecast indicated a continuation of today's weather: blue skies and steady winds, perfect conditions for venturing out onto the bay from Nassau Point in *Tineff*, his little sailboat.

He was alone at the cottage, the way he liked it. His secretary Helen Dukas, also his housekeeper since the death of his second wife, Elsa, in 1936, had remained behind in Princeton. But solitude and sailing plans were likely to be disrupted by tomorrow's visitors.

Albert had been tempted to reject the visit, order that it be postponed until he returned to New Jersey at the end of the season. But fellow physicist Niels Bohr had urged him not to dawdle and to meet with the two men as soon as possible. The situation in Europe not only grew more perilous by the day as indicated by the radio and newspaper reports, there were darker rumblings on the horizon, Nazi threats as yet unrevealed to the public at large. Niels felt they could not risk delaying.

Needing a distraction from the troubles and tensions that tomorrow's visitors likely would bring, Albert settled into his comfortable leather chair beside an open window and delved into a book. He'd borrowed it from a neighbor, an aspiring sculptor. The book was a far cry from his usual fare, which tended to be steeped in the rigors of science and higher mathematics.

It was a brief history of the 1913 International Exhibition of Modern Art, a touring show that began its successful run at a Manhattan armory before proceeding to venues in Chicago and Boston. The show had served to introduce experimental European styles such as Cubism and Futurism to American audiences. A number of artists had achieved fame through the exhibition with their unusual works, most prominently Henri Matisse and Marcel Duchamp.

The book included a number of photographic plates of the artists' projects. Albert had never been enamored with the modern art scene. Matisse's portraits, *Blue Nude* and *Madras Rouge*, left him cold. Yet he couldn't help but admit that Duchamp's *Nude Descending a Staircase, No. 2* possessed a quality that defied simple analysis and subsequent dismissal. The painting's sense of abstract motion – delineated by cones and cylinders in shades of gold, ochre and brown – seemed to render it simultaneously irrational and logical. The Frenchman's effort had captured, in artistic form, the paradoxes that might or might not be inherent to the pesky and oft indigestible impacts of quantum theory.

He stared at the painting, trying to make sense out of it, trying to see something beyond the mere image. Suddenly, a newborn baby materialized swathed in an inner light that brought to mind the multi-hued luminosity of a brilliant sunrise. She floated a few feet away, just beyond his reach. Was he dreaming? If so, the dream bore a potency he had never experienced. Sitting up, he tentatively extended a hand to touch the tiny figure. But at the moment contact should have occurred, the apparition disappeared.

Albert was puzzled yet too tired to contemplate. His youth was behind him, having turned sixty in March, and his waking energy level had decreased even as his mass had increased. He supposed there was a formula linking a person's tiredness with their age and rotundity. If so, he was not the man to seek it. Still, on the surface it would seem that such a theoretical formula was an inverse of $E=mc^2$, whereby even a modest increase in mass could lead to a tremendous increase in energy.

Thinking of his famous equation ignited fresh concerns about tomorrow's visitors and the purpose of their meeting. How a thing so elegant as a formula relating mass, energy and the speed of light could become, some thirty years later, the basis for such troubles was a thing he'd never contemplated. Yet perhaps that belief wasn't entirely true. Perhaps his subconscious mind indeed had noted the possibility decades ago but had refused to allow it full entry into awareness, except maybe in his darkest dreams.

He closed the book and headed for the bedroom. Leo Szilárd, who had produced a nuclear chain reaction at a Columbia University lab, would arrive in less than twelve hours, accompanied by the occasionally volatile Edward Teller. Albert knew exactly what they wanted of him. He was to dictate a letter, already primarily composed by Szilárd and other fellow physicists, to President Franklin D. Roosevelt. Szilárd felt that the letter would carry more impact if it came from Einstein, arguably the world's most famous scientist.

The letter would warn that it was becoming probable, based on the recent experimental work by Szilárd and others, for a chain reaction to be set up in a large mass of uranium. Such an event could unleash a vast amount of power and create large quantities of new radium-like elements. It could allow for the construction of bombs so powerful that should one be carried by a ship into a port, detonation could destroy the entire port as well as the surrounding territory.

The letter would note that Germany had stopped the sale of uranium from the Czechoslovakian mines it has taken over, and that American research on uranium was now being replicated by German physicists at Kaiser-Wilhelm-Institut in Berlin. To counter the inevitable conclusion that the Nazis were attempting to develop such a weapon, the United States should start its own nuclear program.

A part of him knew that the letter to Roosevelt was the right thing to do. They could not take the chance of Germany building such a bomb first. Still, another part of him nurtured doubts. He could envision a future where such atomic weapons might result in unprecedented levels of global destruction, perhaps even to the point where the human species itself would court extinction. That was good enough reason for *not* putting his signature to such a document.

One way or another, the dilemma would resolve itself tomorrow. He'd expended enough thought on it this evening. He got into bed, pulled a light cover up to his neck and turned out the lights.

But just as sleep seemed ready to close its net, something utterly strange happened. He couldn't be sure of the reality of what was happening, but it seemed as if a naked woman lay nestled in bed beside him.

Was she real? Or was he was experiencing an intense dream, one in which perceptions were being lensed to such a degree that the very fabric of consciousness was warped.

The woman leaned over him, pressed her bosom against his chest. Her body gave off a swaddling energy. Her skin emitted a pleasantly tart aroma, reminding him of freshly peeled apples fated for crust and oven. The whisper of her breath tickled the brittle hairs of his neck. Her fingers delved under his nightshirt, probing and caressing.

He felt himself growing excited. The reaction served to ground the experience in the realm of the authentic. It was not a dream, not a fantasy. She felt real therefore had to be real. And yet at the same time, he knew that this could not be the case.

Whatever she was, her kinetic presence triggered a memory from more than three decades ago, when he'd worked in that patent office in Bern, Switzerland. He'd been tasked with examining the plans for The Zurich Electrical Supply Company's invention for promoting feminine relaxation and improved health, their Premium Vibrator. Back then, he'd believed that however pleasurable such a creation, it could not compare to the organic prototype upon which it was based.

But the years had dulled such certainty, and he now acknowledged that no proof existed to support the claim, and that such a belief might represent little more than relativistic prejudice, the thrusting expression of Albert's maleness.

She kissed the lobe of his ear, gently ran her mouth down across his cheek. Her tongue probed his lips. Their faces blended with a passion born of both familiarity and new discovery. They made love with tender urgency, a climbing couplet, swirling into and around one another, seeking and retreating. Yet as with a swirl of two noble gases that could never truly join atomic structures to form a compound, a distance remained between them, a gap that he sensed the woman refused to, or was unable to, cross.

She left him as quickly as she'd arrived, slipping out of bed and dissolving into a blur of shadows beyond the nightstand. Not until that moment did he suspect that she must have been the same woman he'd encountered on the bench outside the Bern patent office in 1905.

On occasion throughout the intervening years, Albert had thought about the phantom woman who'd called herself Stella. He'd never been able to escape the notion that her appearance and interaction with him had shortly thereafter led to the final development and publication of some of his most important theories. Special relativity, the photoelectric effect and, most germane to the letter to Roosevelt he was expected to sign, his paper on inertia and energy content. That introduction of $E=mc^2$ into the lexicon of physics and popular imagination had jump-started international efforts to unleash the energy of the atom. Could all of it in some unfathomable way have been inspired by Stella?

No physical evidence remained to prove she'd actually been there and engaged in the sex act with him. Nevertheless, a feeling of serenity and post-coital languor came over Albert. Lying there in bed he felt more at peace than he had in a long time, more attuned to the moment, less concerned about distant possibilities, about the far future.

Indeed, the development of nuclear bombs might someday threaten all of humanity. There was no getting around that possibility. Yet the insatiable Nazi war machine existed on a closer temporal horizon and represented a more immediate and fundamental threat.

He drifted into a sleep devoid of dreams, secure in the knowledge that tomorrow he would sign the letter.

* * * * *

Sexual liaisons with Einstein and Duchamp were aspects of her plan but introducing distortions into the future of the human species was not. It was an unavoidable side effect. Certain patterns had been set in motion that unlikely would have happened without her intervention. Even trapped here amid these self- aware organic entities grown of the DNA she remained, to a large extent, a creature apart, a creature of pure intellect. And yet...

Something strange was happening to her, something that defied the very nature of her normal observational identity, albeit an identity removed from its natural habitat. Rationally, she understood. Caught up in this locus enabled the conditions for bidirectional impact to occur.

Such a result had happened before of course, countless times. The pattern was a well-established aspect of her existence and should not have surprised her.

But it always did. It always felt new.

Just as she was capable of influencing Duchamp and Einstein, they were capable of influencing her, albeit on levels beneath those of intellectual consciousness. She was being swayed by the corporeal. Psychic turmoil was being planted by the erratic energies inherent to Anomalous Tripartites. Turbulent forces of physicality and emotionality were undercutting the purity of objective analysis, creating imbalances that were simultaneously exciting and disturbing.

Was this the sort of chaotic agitation that humans experienced throughout their existence? If so, how did the species survive? Did they possess some organizing principle opaque to her own perspective that allowed them to maintain a steady course and function in the midst of near-constant turbulence? Did they unconsciously recognize that mass-casualty warfare was a suitable means for maintaining long-term stability?

The questions lacked clear answers, perhaps because she was becoming too much like them. She was losing her ability to perceive the situation from a strictly rational point of view. Her manipulation of Duchamp and Einstein, whether physical, emotional or some combination of the two, was causing her to entertain upsetting ideas, including a sense of guilt that she was negatively impacting the entire future of their species.

Was it really necessary for her to escape the limitations of Duchamp's lifestream? Did not his span of years offer an opportunity for numerous interactions with artists possessed of similar brilliance? Were not John Cage, James Joyce, Langston Hughes, Billie Holiday and Frida Kahlo equally worthy of physical and emotional entanglements?

Would it really be so bad to be marooned here indefinitely, utilizing gifted humans to perpetually refuel?

No, a permanent fusion was incomprehensible. She was a visitor to a realm of Anomalous Tripartites, not an immigrant. Disengagement was vital despite her contrary desires to deepen involvement. Besides, the amalgamation had been realized. Having ensnared both Duchamp and Einstein made the expulsion inevitable. And her subsequent departure was part of the pattern.

Albert Einstein awoke in a daze and could not recall where he had previously been. Nor was he familiar with his current surroundings. It was possible he was still in some sort of dream state.

Yet even dreams have rules, he thought. Freud had claimed that dreams liberate us from the constraints of matter. Yet Albert sensed he was fettered, as if some force more powerful than electromagnetism bound him to this place.

He seemed to be standing in a windowless study in front of a high bookcase crammed with texts. Across the room was a green couch and large oak desk with an antique navigation sextant resting upon it. In the far corner, a cushioned armchair of rich dark leather suggested luxurious comfort.

He returned his attention to the bookcase. Many of the texts were in Spanish, a language he couldn't read. At random he pulled a book from the shelf. Judging by its cover, a yellow frog in a tropical forest, it seemed to be about amphibians.

And then something more startling caught his attention. His own hand. The flesh was taut, free of the age lines and liver spots indicative of his advanced years.

Running his fingers across his face and through his hair provided further evidence of a pleasing alteration. The skin was smooth, the hair short and barely touching his ears. He plucked a strand from his scalp. Even in the dim illumination he could see that it was black, not white.

He was young again.

Movement. Across the study. A man shifted his position in the armchair, which Einstein was certain had been unoccupied only moments before. The man looked vaguely familiar.

Marcel Duchamp awakened, surprised at his locale and unable to remember where he had been prior to this comfortable chair. The figure standing by the bookcase at the other end of the room grabbed his attention. The man looked very much like that famed physicist, Albert Einstein, albeit a younger version than pictured in recent newspaper photos.

Marcel arose and as he did, became aware of something extraordinary. The varied and distasteful infirmities of aging had departed, replaced by the energetic bounties of youth.

He stared at the scientist. "What has happened? Where am I?"

"I was rather hoping you would tell me."

"Is this another of Salvador's jokes?" Duchamp wondered. In some undefinable way, the environment reeked of Dali's impishness.

The Dali comment sparked Einstein's memory. The man was Marcel Duchamp, the noted artist. They'd had a brief encounter decades ago in Prague. He too appeared not to have aged.

Duchamp's attention was drawn to the wall beside the bookcase, to an impressive reproduction of Diego Velazquez's 1656 painting, *Las Meninas*. Strangely, the rectangular mirror in the painting's background, a portrait of King Philip IV and Queen Mariana of Spain, seemed to be real. In it he could see his own reflection superimposed upon the image of the royals.

The king and queen came alive. With the jerky movement of marionettes, they pivoted and dashed away. Their retreating figures shriveled to miniscule dots against a blurred horizon.

A fierce light filled the mirror, so intense it seemed as if the sun itself was burning within the glass. Duchamp was forced to shield his eyes.

Einstein had an angled view of the painting. From his perspective, the unnatural light flowing from the mirror seemed to curve toward him, as if some invisible gravitational body of immense proportions was warping its journey. Its brightness caused him to avert his gaze.

The blinding light vanished. In its place, Stella, in a shimmering dress of many colors, stepped out of the mirror's frame and into the room. Einstein recognized her from his two previous encounters, or at least from the two he could remember. Had she interacted with him on other occasions over the years that he couldn't recall?

"It is good to see you again, Stella," he offered, unsure of his own sincerity even as he uttered the words. She was clearly a transformative entity, capable of spatiotemporal achievements that transcended his theoretical understanding of the universe. Yet she was also a lover capable of endowing a partner with remarkable feelings of serenity. He judged it best to compliment rather than criticize.

"Salut," Duchamp said in his native French. His ethereal muse – or more properly, *their* ethereal muse judging by Einstein's reaction – also appeared not to have aged. Perhaps she was like a Readymade work of art, forever frozen in the instant of its creation.

"Good evening, gentleman. Welcome to this actuality."

"A place that would seem to exist in violation of scientific principles," Einstein proposed.

"It seems neither dream nor hallucination but something else entirely," Duchamp said.

"Your inquisitiveness is understandable. But perhaps you could contain your queries. I have a proposition."

Stella walked to the center of the study, to a small table with a chess board that Einstein was certain had not been there a moment ago. Flanking the table were a pair of straight-backed wooden chairs. A chandelier appeared above to cast a warm glow upon the kings and queens, bishops and knights, rooks and pawns, all properly aligned for the start of a match.

"I promised you both a game."

"And I recall that moment," Einstein said. "Yet surely you don't expect us to just sit down and play chess without further explanation."

"He makes a good point," Duchamp said.

"The explanation is contained in the playing of the game."

Duchamp glanced at Einstein, saw no objection and nodded to Stella. "Is there a prize for the winner?"

"Only the inherent satisfaction of victory over a worthy opponent."

"A curious proposition," Einstein said. "However, I understand that Duchamp is a most accomplished player whereas I remain a mere amateur."

"While that may be true," Duchamp countered, "your analytical prowess is unmatched." He turned to Stella. "It would be foolish to underestimate his chess abilities. But in the spirit of fairness, I am open to playing with a handicap of two pawns."

"It will not be necessary to remove any pieces from their starting positions. In this game, each of you will have one chance to create a new rule. If I deem the rule fair, the chess board shall transform accordingly. Your suggestions must appeal to my sensibilities and not produce near-instantaneous victory, but otherwise be without limitations. You may request the most unorthodox of ideas. Surrealist excursions into the impossible, the bending of time and space… whatever your bodies and hearts desire."

Einstein nodded in acceptance of the challenge. "Creating rules has always been a passion."

"And breaking them is mine," Duchamp added, taking a seat at the table.

Einstein assumed the opposite position and studied his opponent's face, well aware of the eccentric artist's skills as an innovative thinker.

Duchamp grabbed a white pawn and, out of Einstein's view, enclosed it in his hand. He extended his fists. "My left or my right?"

"Your right."

Duchamp opened his right fist, revealing the pawn.

"Good luck," Einstein said, replacing the piece alongside its comrades.

"To you as well."

"Begin," Stella instructed.

A dual-faced chess clock appeared beside the board, ticking like a muffled metronome.

Einstein moved his white King's Pawn two squares forward. Duchamp moved his Queen's Bishop one square forward, invoking the well-known nineteenth-century Caro-Kann Defense. Einstein moved his Queen's Pawn forward two, and Duchamp followed suit with his Queen's Pawn.

Einstein chose the exchange variation as his pawn took Duchamp's, who in turn recaptured with his own pawn. Einstein moved his King's Bishop to queen Three.

A few moves later, Einstein offered his King's Knight as a sacrifice with the hope of gaining the initiative.

"I see that you wish to inject some fresh blood into this old line," Duchamp said. "Even in chess, things are not always black and white."

Following the cautious opening dance, they parried each other's threats and initiated new lines of attack. Each began to experience the sensation that their minds were synchronizing and that they were anticipating one another's thoughts. Einstein wondered whether their intertwining intellects could generate an infinitely growing feedback loop. Duchamp wondered if Stella's grand game was to cross-fertilize their collective unconscious through the medium of chess, perhaps to interlink art and science.

Their muse stood off the side, silently observing.

Neither man perceived the passage of time: their focus was entirely on the game. Pieces were moved cautiously or with swift certainty. Threats were made and dodged. The chess clock ticked onward.

Following a grueling chase, Duchamp was able to capture Einstein's menacing knight. Despite his material advantage, Duchamp's king was in an exposed and perilous state. He began to feel anxious about missing out on the spoils for the victor, that potential moment of transcendent insight.

"I propose the rule that we activate the duality of gender, and that Einstein and I have our kings and queens transform into one another."

Stella hesitated for the briefest moment then nodded. "Your appeal is accepted."

She waved her hand at the board, altering it accordingly. Duchamp's previously endangered king found itself in the comfort of his queenside pawns. He breathed a sigh of relief.

They continued to play. Duchamp traded his knight for Einstein's bishop and, perceiving that he had the advantage, sensed a tactical opportunity. He leaned his chin on his palm and studied the position carefully. He knew that he would have to get rid of Einstein's second, equally troublesome knight. If he sacrificed his rook for the knight, a few moves later Einstein's queen would be put in jeopardy.

After additional minutes of deep thought, a plan emerged. Duchamp played rook captures knight.

Einstein studied the move and projected the future ramifications of capturing Duchamp's rook. The loss of material was inevitable. After losing his queen, Einstein's pieces were gradually eliminated. The only remaining pieces were the two kings and Duchamp's queen.

Unwilling to concede defeat, Einstein turned to Stella with a bold suggestion.

"I propose that we transpose colors. Black becomes white and white becomes black."

"Unfair," Duchamp protested.

Stella agreed with the artist. "The recommendation is denied."

Einstein contemplated another escape plan. Knowing that space and energy are intertwined, he realized that if the finite could expand, his king might find a new trajectory.

"Just as our universe is both finite and infinite, I'd like to invoke a new rule. I propose that the edges of this board expand unto infinity such that the board will no longer have any borders."

"Also unfair," Duchamp said.

"Your request is deemed fair, and is accepted."

Within the space of a heartbeat, the study vanished. Along with Stella, Einstein and Duchamp found themselves floating above a chessboard that extended in every direction as far as their eyes could see.

Even knowing it was hopeless, Duchamp moved his Queen and checked Einstein's King, which in turn retreated. This chase proceeded for a little while longer, until Duchamp couldn't hide his disappointment.

"It is impossible to checkmate you with only a queen and king if there is no edge to the board, as you will always be able to keep running away. I concede that the game is a draw."

"Agreed," Einstein said, turning to Stella. "Given the unorthodox nature of the game and the transformative rules you've allowed, I suspect that any match would be destined to end without a winner."

"Which suggests," Duchamp added, "that as players we never had free will, that the game was rigged from the start."

Stella smiled and vanished. The infinite chess board converted into a black featureless plane.

* * * * *

She stood in the darkness on the desert floor, poised to witness the first of this day's two sunrises from a perspective not possible for humans. The four-legged steel tower rose a hundred feet above her; the pre-dawn air was crisp and cool, and endowed with faintest of breezes. A thunderstorm with heavy rain had struck several hours earlier, forcing the experiment to be postponed. But now it was time: July 15, 1945. The detonation would occur at 05:29:45 hours.

Considering her interactions with the two lifestreams – Duchamp and Einstein – it seemed fitting that the test in this isolated area of New Mexico was called Trinity.

Whatever guilt might have plagued her about her role in sending destructive ripples through the bipedals' future had been vanquished before she'd arrived here in the desert. Guilt was a byproduct of the physical and emotional upheaval brought on by her interactions with the two men.

The chess game had been the key to reversing those effects. Concentrating on the game had freed her from her growing addiction to the ways of the humans. The match had helped restore her intellectual focus, thus lessening the influences of physicality and emotionality induced by being trapped in Duchamp and Einstien's lifestream.

The realigning of consciousness into its proper and familiar framework rendered the attractions of being marooned, as well as the contaminating influence of guilt, less troubling.

Rockets were fired into the darkness from afar to signal the event. A distant siren wailed a last warning. Bunkers filled with specialized instruments 800 yards from the tower would measure the flash, heat, radiation and shock impact. Other instruments were situated overhead, suspended by weather balloon or parachuted from aircraft.

The closest humans would bear witness from bunkers 10,000 yards away.

However, many of the Manhattan Project's scientists and engineers, those who had actually designed and built the bomb, were observing from safer distances.

She could sense their presence. Some were slathering faces and arms with a final coating of sunblock, and donning thick dark glasses prior to aiming their binoculars and telescopes in her direction. None would be able to see her, of course. At most they might perceive a vague shadow or a swirl of sand, or perhaps experience an amorphous tingling as their magnifying devices focused on the spot occupied by her non-corporeal essence.

Einstein was not among the observers. The man whose theories and letter to President Roosevelt were pivotal in making the test possible had been considered a security risk and kept in the dark about the development of the atomic bomb. In his later years he would come to regret the letter, claiming that if he'd known the Germans *would fail to develop the bomb he never would have lifted a finger.*

But he had. He couldn't have helped it. Ultimately, none of the humans could have. It was not their fate, not something preordained. It was simply the fullest expression of their identity.

From far away, an order was barked, a signal issued, a circuit closed. The detonators triggered. Directly above her, the bomb ignited.

The flash of light came first, followed an instant later by an expanding eruption of fire. Any organic lifestream in her spot would have been reduced to vapor. Her proximity dictated a different outcome.

The blast ascended in a billowing cloud to 8,000 feet in the fraction of a second.

The expanding fireball, a rage of chromatic mutation, swiftly climbed higher, punched through the clouds above. A thunderous roar shook the ground. A thermal windstorm cascaded across the desert, destroying everything in its path.

The humans' first atomic detonation would be measured as equivalent to 18,600 tons of conventional explosives, enough energy to meet her dual objectives. Later bombs thousands of times more powerful would be responsible for wiping out the majority of the species.

The bomb's energy reversed the effects of her faux-physicality, freed her from the finite yesterdays and tomorrows of Duchamp's lifestream. Disengagement, her first objective, was an unqualified success. She was propelled back into her native form, a pure observational context.

From her restored perspective, she turned her attention back to the nuclear cloud ascending into the early morning heavens. Employing senses beyond human capacity, she looked deep into that mushrooming cascade in order to bear witness to her second objective, the expulsion, an ethereal bundle of luminescence birthed within fires too hot for any mortal to survive.

The glowing infant was only the latest in a totality of expulsions stretching back through the existence of the universe. Vague memories of previous expulsions touched her, all part of that repeating pattern consisting of fascination with an Anomalous Tripartite world, entrapment in a lifestream and sexual liaison with a partner or partners to fertilize her seed. Those seeds, planted amid countless Anomalous Tripartite species, might grow into adults who drastically altered the direction of their civilization, although it was just as likely that an expulsion lived its short life with no discernible impact upon planetary events.

Had she still been trapped in Duchamp's lifestream, she supposed she might have acknowledged a preference for one of those possibilities. But she felt nothing for the infant, neither passionate need or desire, nor any other type of human emotion typifying the mother-child bond. The only matter that concerned her was that the expulsion not perish amid nuclear vapors.

To that end she snatched the core of its unripened consciousness from the incinerating fires and transferred it into the nearest survivable habitat forty miles away, the womb of a migrant farmer's wife, surname Rodriguez. The woman was on the verge of delivering her first child.

The newborn girl emerged, crying heartily. The midwife cleaned and cradled it, and cut the cord. An instant later, mother and nurse raised their eyes in tandem to the bedroom window, gazing into the darkness in wonderment at the strange distant light.

Her task accomplished, she turned her attention back to the superheated air above ground zero. The mushroom cloud reached its apex and began to wither. Soon it would be gone. Soon the day's second sunrise, however brief, would come upon the desert.

THE END

APPENDIX 1

Princteon, USA 1933
White Albert Einstein
Black Robert Oppenheimer

1. e4 e5
2. Nf3 Nc6
3. Bb5 a6
4. Ba4 b5
5. Bb3 Nf6
6. O-O Nxe4
7. Re1 d5
8. a4 {Nc3 or d3 would have been stronger.}
   8...b4 {Black should have replied ...Bc5}
9. d3 Nc5 {retreating with Nf6 is better}
10. Nxe5 Ne7
11. Qf3 f6 {Be6 still held some hope for Black}
12. Qh5+ g6

13. Nxg6 hxg6
14. Qxh8 Nxb3
15. cxb3 Qd6
16. Bh6 and Black resigned. 1-0

Hyères, France 1928
White:Marcel Duchamp
Black: E. H. Smith

1. d4 d5
2. Nf3 Nf6
3. c4 e6
4. Nc3 b6
5. cxd5 Nxd5 {recapturing with the pawn is
    more common}
6. Bd2 Ba6
7. Ne5 Nxc3
8. Bxc3 f6 9.e3!? {Duchamp plays aggressively
    and offers to sacrifice material for an attack.
    While this is not the best move, it certainly is
    creative.}

9. ...fxe5? {Smith falters here. Stronger would have been to continue 9...BxB 10.Qh5+ g6 11. Nxg6 hxN 12.Qxg6 Kd7 RxB where white has compensation for the sacrificed material.}
10. Bxa6 Nxa6
11. a4+ Qd7 {Instead of 11.. Qd7 the move ..c6 was equally playable and after white takes the knight on a6, the position is also slightly in white's favor.}
12. Qxa6 Be7? {there was no need to give up a free pawn. Smith should have played pawn takes pawn.}
13. dxe5 O-O {Now white's advantage is signficant.}
14. O-O c5
15. Rad1 Qc7
16. Qc4 Qc6
17. a4 Rad8
18. f4 Rxd1
19. Rxd1 g6

20. Rd6! {A brilliant final blow, which breaks Black's fortress.} 20...Bxd6
21. Qxe6+ Rf7
22. exd6 Qd7
23. Qe5 White's advantage is overwhelming and Black resigned. 1-0

APPENDIX 2

Albert Einstein
Old Grove Rd.
Nassau Point
Peconic, Long Island

August 2nd, 1939

F.D. Roosevelt,
President of the United States,
White House
Washington, D.C.

Sir:

Some recent work by E. Fermi and L. Szilard, which has been communicated to me in manuscript, leads me to expect that the element uranium may be turned into a new and important source of energy in the immediate future. Certain aspects of the situation which has arisen seem to call for watchfulness and, if necessary, quick action on the part of the Administration. I believe therefore that it is my duty to bring to your attention the following facts and recommendations:

In the course of the last four months it has been made probable - through the work of Joliot in France as well as Fermi and Szilard in America - that it may become possible to set up a nuclear chain reaction in a large mass of uranium, by which vast amounts of power and large quantities of new radium-like elements would be generated. Now it appears almost certain that this could be achieved in the immediate future.

This new phenomenon would also lead to the construction of bombs, and it is conceivable - though much less certain - that extremely powerful bombs of a new type may thus be constructed. A single bomb of this type, carried by boat and exploded in a port, might very well destroy the whole port together with some of the surrounding territory. However, such bombs might very well prove to be too heavy for transportation by air.

The United States has only very poor ores of uranium in moderate quantities. There are some good ores In Canada and the former Czechoslovakia, while the most important source of uranium is Belgian Congo.

In view of the situation you may think it desirable to have some permanent contact maintained between the administration and the group of physicists working on chain reactions in America. One possible way of achieving this might be for you to entrust with this task a person who has your confidence and who could perhaps serve in an inofficial capacity. His task might comprise the following:

a) to approach Government Departments, keep them informed of the further development, and put forward recommendations for government action, giving particular attention to the problem of securing a supply of uranium ore for the United States;

b) to speed up the experimental work, which is at present being carried on within the limits of the budgets of University laboratories, by providing funds, if such funds be required, through his contacts with private persons who are willing to make contributions for this cause, and perhaps also by obtaining the co-operation of industrial laboratories which have the necessary equipment.

I understand that Germany has actually stopped the sale of uranium from the Czechoslovakian mines which she has taken over. That she should have taken such early action might perhaps be understood on the ground that the son of the German Under-Secretary of state, von Weiszäcker, is attached to the Kaiser-Wilhelm-Institut in Berlin where some of the American work on uranium is now being repeated.

Yours very truly,
A. Einstein

The White House
Washington
October 19, 1939

My dear Professor:

I want to thank you for your recent letter and the most interesting and important enclosure.

I found this data of such import that I have convened a Board consisting of the head of the Bureau of Standards and a chosen representative of the Army and Navy to thoroughly investigate the possibilities of your suggestion regarding the element of uranium.

I am glad to say that Dr. Sachs will cooperate and work with this Committee and I feel that this is the most practical and effective method of dealing with the subject.

Please accept my sincere thanks.

Very sincerely yours,
Franklin D. Roosevelt

EXCLUSIVE FIRST CHAPTER
OF STARSHIP ALCHEMON
FROM CHRISTOPHER HINZ

STARSHIP
ALCHEMON

CHRISTOPHER HINZ

CHAPTER 1

The assignor had a hunch the meeting would be unpleasant. He wondered if the young woman entering his office already knew the outcome.

LeaMarsa de Host wore a black skirt and sweater that looked woven from rags, clothing surely lacking even basic hygiene nanos. Whether she was making some sort of anti-Corporeal statement or whether she always dressed like a drug-addled misfit from the Helio Age was not apparent from her file.

The assignor smiled and rose to shake her hand. She ignored the courtesy. He sat and motioned her to the chair across from his desk.

"Welcome to Pannis Corp, LeaMarsa."

"Thrilled to be here."

Her words bled sarcasm. No surprise. She registered highly alienated on the Ogden Tripartite Thought Ordination. Most members of the bizarre minority to which she belonged were outliers on the OTTO scale.

"Would you like something to drink?" he asked, motioning to his Starbucks 880, a conglomeration of tubes and spouts. The dispenser was vintage twenty-first-century, a gift from the assignor's wife for his thirtieth birthday. "Five hundred and one varieties, hot or cold."

"I'll have a juggernaut cocktail with Europa cryospice. Hold the cinnamon."

"I'm sorry, that one's not in the menu."

She grimaced with disappointment, which of course was the whole point of requesting such a ridiculously exotic drink.

He unflexed his wafer to max screen size and toggled through her file. An analysis of her test results appeared.

"The Pannis researchers at Jamal Labs were most impressed with your talents. You are indeed a gifted psionic."

She flopped into the chair and leaned back. An erratic thumping reverberated through the office. It took the assignor a moment to realize she was kicking the underside of his desk with the toe of her flats.

He contained his annoyance. Someday, he hoped to have enough seniority to avoid working with her type. And this young woman in particular...

She was thin, with long dark hair hanging to her shoulders, grossly uncouth. His preadolescent daughter still wore her hair that long, but who beyond the teen years allowed such draping strands, and LeaMarsa de Host was twenty three. Her skin was as pale as the froth of a milkshake and her eyes hard blue gems, constantly probing. She smelled of natural body scents. He didn't care for the odor.

"Let's cut to the chase," she said. "Do I get a starship?"

"At this time, Pannis Corp feels that such an assignment would not be in the best interests of all involved."

"What's the matter? Afraid?"

He'd been trained to ignore such a response. "Pannis has concluded that your particular range of abilities would not be conducive to the self-contained existence of stellar voyaging."

"What the hell does that mean?"

"It boils down to a matter of cooperation."

"Haven't I cooperated with your tests? I took two months out of my life. I practically lived in those hideous Jamal Labs of yours."

"And we're certainly pleased by your sacrifice. But when I'm speaking of cooperation, I'm referring to factors of which you may not even be conscious. Psionic abilities exist primarily in strata beneath the level of daily awareness."

"Really? Never would have guessed."

He paved over the snark. "You may wish to behave cooperatively but find your subconscious acting in contrary ways. And trust me, a year or more in a starship is a far cry from what you underwent in our labs."

"You're speaking from experience?"

"Actually, no. I've never been farther out than Luna."

"Then you don't know what you're talking about."

She stared at him so intently that he worried she was trying to read his mind. The fear was irrational. Still, like most of the population, he was categorized as a psionic receptor, susceptible to psychic forces, albeit mildly.

He forced attention back to the wafer.

"Pannis is willing to offer you a choice of more than a dozen positions, all with good salary ranges. And the benefits of working for a mega are remarkable."

"What's the most exciting position?"

"Exciting? Why, I don't know." He tapped the wafer, scanned pages. "Ah yes, here's one that sounds quite exciting. Archeological assistant, digging up ninteenth century frontier cultures in the American southwest in search of lost caches of gold and silver."

"Blizzards?"

He looked up from the wafer. "Pardon?"

"Do you have anything with blizzards? I like storms."

Storms? Dear god, these people were a trial, and more trouble than they were worth. Still, he understood the economics behind the current frenzy among Pannis and the other megas to employ them.

Only last week the latest discovery attributed to one of LeaMarsa's kind had been announced, a metallic compound found in the swamps of the dwarf planet Buick Skylark. The mega funding that expedition, Koch-Fox, was touting the compound as key ingredient for a new construction material impervious to the effects of sunlight.

He scanned more pages on the wafer. "Yes, here's a position where storms factor in. The south polar regions, an industrial classification. You would utilize your abilities to locate ultra-deep mineral deposits."

"While freezing my butt off? No thanks. Anyway, no need to read further. I've made my decision."

"Excellent."

"I choose a starship."

The assignor couldn't hide his disappointment. "Again, you must understand that a starship is not in the best interests of…"

He trailed off as the door slid open. An immaculately dressed man with dark hair and a weightlifter's build strolled in. He wore a gray business suit with matching headband. A pewter-colored vest rose to his chin and a dwarf lion perched on his shoulder, a male judging by its thick mane. The cat couldn't have weighed more than two pounds. A genejob that small cost more than the assignor earned in a year.

The man was a high-ranking Pannis official, the InterGlobal Security VP, a rank rarely seen on this floor of the Manhattan office complex. His name was Renfro Zoobondi and he was hardcore, an up-and-comer known and feared throughout the corporation.

The fact that Zoobondi was here filled the assignor with dread.

A black mark, he thought bitterly. *I'm not handling this situation correctly and my file will soon reflect that.*

Zoobondi must have been monitoring their conversation, which suggested that LeaMarsa was even more important than her dazzling psionic ratings indicated. The VP was here to rectify the assignor's failure.

He won't come right out and criticize me. That's not the Pannis way. He'll say I've done a fair job under difficult circumstances and then see to it I'm given a black mark.

Zoobondi sat on the edge of the assignor's desk and faced LeaMarsa. The diminutive lion emitted a tinny growl.

"You are being uncooperative, Mizz de Host." The VP's voice was deep and commanding.

She shrugged. He regarded her for a long moment then turned to the assignor.

"Access vessel departures. Look for a minor mission, something leaving within the next few weeks."

The assignor did as asked while cloaking surprise. *Is he actually considering such an unstable individual for a starship?*

Zoobondi wagged a finger at LeaMarsa. "Understand me, young lady, you will not be given a major assignment. But Pannis is prepared to gratify."

The assignor called up the file. He scanned the lengthy list, narrowed down the possibilities.

"The *Bolero Grand*, two-year science project, galactic archaeology research. Crew of sixty-eight, including two lytics—"

"Perhaps something smaller," Zoobondi suggested, favoring her with a smile. "We want Mizz de Host to enjoy the special bonding that can develop aboard vessels with a minimal number of shipmates."

"Yes, of course. How about the *Regis*, crew of six? Fourteen-month mission to Pepsi One in the HD 40307 system. They're laying the groundwork for new colonies and request a psionic to help select the best geographic locations on the semi-liquid surface."

"Perfect. Does that work for you, LeaMarsa?"

"No. Sounds boring."

"It does, doesn't it," Zoobondi said with a smile. "I'd certainly get bored traipsing across a world of bubbling swamps looking for seismic stability."

The assignor was confused. Something was going on here that he didn't understand. If Zoobondi wanted her to accept the *Regis* mission, he would have made it sound more attractive.

"Any other possibilities?" the VP asked.

"Yes. Starship *Alchemon*, eighteen-month mission to the Lalande 21185 system. Investigation of an anomalous biosignature discovered by an unmanned probe. Crew of eight, including a lytic."

Zoobondi shook his head. "I don't think so."

"Why not?" LeaMarsa demanded.

He hesitated, as if working on a rebuttal. The assignor understood.

He wants her to accept this mission. He's leading her along. The assignor had been with Pannis long enough to recognize applied reverse psychology, which meant that this meeting with LeaMarsa was part of a high-level setup.

It was possible he wouldn't get a black mark after all. "Departing lunar orbit in seven days," he continued, following the VP's lead. "They'll be landing on the fifth planet, Sycamore, where the probe found evidence of bacterial life. It's a violently unstable world, locked in perpetual storms."

He glanced up at LeaMarsa, expecting the presence of storms to produce a reaction. He wasn't disappointed.

"Sounds perfect. I want it."

The VP adopted a thoughtful look, as if pretending to consider her demand. The dwarf lion rubbed its mane against his ear, seeking attention. Zoobondi ignored the animal.

"Where do I sign?" LeaMarsa pressed.

"Would you please wait in the lobby."

She strode out with that stiffly upright gait that seemed to characterize so many psionics. Renfro

Zoobondi held his tongue until the door whisked shut behind her.

"You'll take care of the details, make sure she's aboard?"

It wasn't really a question.

"Yes sir. But I do have some concerns."

The assignor hesitated, unsure how forthright he should be. This was obviously a setup. For reasons above his security clearance, Pannis wanted LeaMarsa on that ship. But dropping a powerful and moody psionic into such a lengthy mission fell outside the guidelines of standard policy, not to mention being enticing bait to some Corporeal prosecuting attorney looking to make a name. He didn't want to be the Pannis fall guy if things went wrong.

"Sir, I feel obligated to point out that LeaMarsa de Host is no ordinary psionic. The Jamal Labs report classifies her in the upper one-ten-thousandth of one percent for humans with such abilities."

"Your point?"

"There are a number of red flags. And the OTTO classifies her as—"

"Most psionics have issues. A long voyage might do her good. Bring her out of her shell."

"She suffers from the occasional loss of consciousness while wide awake, a condition the Jamal researchers term 'psychic blackouts.' Even more disturbing, she's been known to inflict bodily harm on herself through self-flagellation or other means. Presumably, she does this as an analgesic against some unknown emotional torment originating in childhood."

The VP looked bored. He stroked the lion's back. The animal hissed.

The assignor tabbed open another part of LeaMarsa's file and made a final stab at getting his concerns across. "Sir, to quote the Jamal analysts, 'LeaMarsa de Host is a disturbing jumble of contradictory emotions. It is imperative that careful consideration be given to placement in order to prevent–'"

"The *Alchemon* is one of the newer ships, isn't it? Full security package?"

"Yes sir, the works. Anti-chronojacker system with warrior pups. And of course, a Level Zero Sentinel."

"A very safe vessel. I don't believe she'll cause any problems that the ship and crew can't handle."

The assignor knew he had to take a stand. "Sir, putting someone like her aboard that ship could create serious issues. And wouldn't it make more sense for her vast talents to be utilized on a mission here on Earth, something with the potential for a more lucrative payoff?"

"Better for her to be first given a less critical assignment to gauge how she handles team interaction."

"Yes sir, that makes sense, but–"

Zoobondi held up a hand for silence. He slid off the edge of the desk and removed a safepad from his pocket, stuck the slim disk to the wall. A faint, low-pitched hum filled the office as the safepad scrambled localized surveillance, rendering their conversation impervious to eavesdropping. The lion squirmed on the VP's shoulder, bothered by the sound.

"We're entering a gray area here," Zoobondi said. "Trust me when I say it's best you don't pursue this subject."

The assignor could only nod. If things indeed went bad, he likely would be the one to take the fall. And there was nothing he could do about it.

Zoobondi smiled and threw him a bone. "I believe you're due for a promotional review next month."

"Yes sir."

"Everything I've read suggests you're doing a fine job. Keep up the good work and I'm certain that your promotion will come through."

The VP deactivated and pocketed the safepad and strolled out the door. The assignor was relieved he was gone. There were dark tales murmured about Renfro Zoobondi. He was ruthlessness personified, supposedly having arranged for the career sabotage of g men and women standing in the path of his climb up the corporate ladder. There was even a rumor that for no other reason than the twisted joy of it, he'd killed a man in armor-suit combat.

The assignor returned to the file on the *Alchemon* expedition. Reading between the lines, he wondered whether researching a primordial lifeform was really the mission's primary purpose. Could Pannis have a different agenda, a hidden one?

He closed the file. If that was the case, there was little to be done. He was midlevel management, an undistinguished position within a massive interstellar corporation. Going against the wishes of a man like Renfro Zoobondi was career suicide. The assignor had a wife and young daughter to consider. What would happen to them if he lost his job and possibly fell into the ranks of the "needful majority," those billions who were impoverished and struggling? It wasn't so farfetched, had happened to a good friend only last month.

That night, the assignor slept fitfully. In the morning he awoke covered in sweat. He'd been in the clutches of a terrifying nightmare.

Thankfully, he couldn't recall any details.

ABOUT THE AUTHORS

ETAN ILFELD is the author of *Beyond Contemporary Art* and graduated at the top of his physics class at Stanford University. He is a US chess master and the inventor of Diving Chess where each player can think for each move as long as they can hold their breath each time. Ilfeld is the founder of Tenderbooks, Repeater Books, and the managing director of Watkins Books and the Mind Sports Olympiad.

CHRISTOPHER HINZ is the author of five science fiction books. *Liege-Killer* won the Compton Crook Award for best first novel and was nominated for the John W. Campbell Award for best new writer. He has written screenplays and a graphic novel, scripted comics for DC and Marvel, and has worked as a newspaper reporter and technical administrator of a small TV station.

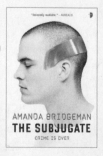